Praise

"Jessica Bell's surprising risks with language capture a child's clear vision in a world of adult heartbreak. Indelible. Courageous."
THAISA FRANK, AUTHOR OF *HEIDEGGER'S GLASSES* AND *ENCHANTMENT*

"This book goes to the head of the class. Matter of fact, it's in a brand new class of its own. Bell's style of writing is bold and innovative, and thoroughly engaging. What's more, she does an outstanding job capturing the voice and thoughts of a very special little girl named Bonnie. Born prematurely, she may be a little "behind" other children her age, but the wisdom in some of her simplistic insights is startling, and often heart-wrenching. At the centre of this tale is the "badly" journal her parents keep, but Bonnie is the shining star, and it is Bonnie who will linger in your mind and heart."
SUSAN FLETT SWIDERSKI, AUTHOR OF *HOT FLASHES & COLD LEMONADE*

"The Book is lovely ... sad and tragic and oh, really? Oh, no! Oh my goodness. Little Bonnie wriggles her way into your heart in the very first diary passage when the reader hears her voice for the first time. She is bright and quirky, a funny and unique child with very normal, messed up parents. Oh the poor children with the messed up parents! This novella was reminiscent of both "Room" and "The Curious Incident of the Dog in the Night Time," ... A great read, an enchanting child, I had tears in my eyes when it ended. I will be looking for more from this author."
LIBBY BROADBENT, AUTHOR OF *THAT THING THAT HAPPENED*

"A curiously captivating read that somehow manages to encapsulate the length and breadth of love and family in one slim volume."
JOSH DONELLAN, AUTHOR OF *ZEB AND THE GREAT RUCKUS*

about the author

Jessica Bell is an Australian award-winning author and poet, writing and publishing coach, and graphic designer who lives in Athens, Greece. In addition to her novels and poetry collections, and her best-selling *Writing in a Nutshell* series, she has published a variety of works online and in literary journals, including *Writer's Digest*.

Jessica is also the Co-Founder and Publisher of *Vine Leaves Press & Literary Journal*, a singer/songwriter/guitarist, a voice-over actor, and a freelance editor and writer for English Language Teaching publishers worldwide such as Macmillan Education and Education First.

Before she started writing she was just a young woman with a "useless" Bachelor of Arts degree and a waitressing job.

Visit Jessica's website: *jessicabellauthor.com*

The Book
Copyright © 2016 Jessica Bell
All rights reserved.

Vine Leaves Press
Melbourne, Victoria, Australia

Second Edition
ISBN-13: 978-1-925417-46-3

First edition published by Vine Leaves Press Australia, 2013

Cover design by Jessica Bell
Interior design by Amie McCracken

National Library of Australia Cataloguing-in-Publication entry (pbk)
Creator: Bell, Jessica Carmen, author.
Title: The book / Jessica Bell.
Edition: 2nd edition.
ISBN: 9781925417463 (paperback)
Subjects: Families--Fiction.
Diaries--Fiction.
Books--Fiction.
Dewey Number: A823.4

the book

jessica bell

Vine Leaves Press
Melbourne, Vic, Australia

To my four parents

part one

love is the beginning

November 12 th, 1978
~Daddy

While lying in Penny's womb, Penny and I would tickle your feet. You didn't like that. But to feel you through Penny's skin was a sensation so fantastic, it made me realise the love I have for you is quite a tangible thing.

__January 12th, 1979__
~Daddy

At 1:15 a.m., at the Austin Hospital, in Melbourne, you were born, my love. I was the lucky one because I held you for most of the time. It was a thrill just to see you open your eyes and look at me. Then I'd show you to Penny and she would smile her smile that has so much love in it. It lingered in the air so thick, yet so light; sometimes I thought I could hear its wings, hear it find the way to our hearts like little Milky Ways exploding in galaxies unknown to us.

It is the most wonderful thing that has ever happened to me—to see you being born, knowing that no-one can replicate you, that you are you alone, and that Penny and I created you.

Two hours later I'm still beaming with happiness—Bonnie Joy Miller—you are ours alone, so beautiful, so delicate. I know that you already know me—I love you so much, I will always love you because you are simply and purely my child and nothing in this entire world can take that away from me or surpass the feeling of love it has engraved into my very skin, my bones, my being.

You are so tiny—2.55 kg. And only thirty-six weeks in gestation. You are my little girl, my daughter; the reason I do everything I do, and will do. So be it, sweetheart; I hope I live up to the ideals and ambitions of fatherhood that I hold for you.

I love you dearly.

September 4th, 1979
~Mummy

Bonnie—just a thought. This morning is cold and glum. You're asleep, finally, after hours of wailing. The doctor said you have colic and I just have to wait for it to pass. I'm thinking of how fast you are growing, how quickly you've developed a character and how wonderful you make me feel when you smile. How can I stay angry, lonely or sad? You are just too precious. Being your mother is the most rewarding occupation. When I feel those tears coming on, I just look at your face, and it helps me keep them hidden until I go to bed at night.

October 10th, 1979
~Mummy

You're ten months old now and today you started being a little daring by trying to pull yourself up on the record player. You giggled as if you knew you'd achieved something. Bonnie you are always on your tip toes—everyone says you're going to be a ballet dancer. I wonder? You are doing so many things now—creeping, sitting, pulling yourself up, but you haven't got one tooth yet. Every time I go cross-eyed, you giggle like there is nothing funnier in the world. I love how simple life is with you.

December 1st, 1979
~Mummy

Bonnie, if over the years you think that John and I argue a lot, I want you to know that I love him very much, without him there wouldn't be a you. But sometimes things don't work out the way we like. Our egos and prides get in the way and then love just becomes another weapon to hurt each other with. We both love you totally and nothing will ever change that and no matter what doubts you may have in your life you need never, not ever! doubt our love for you.

It's nearly Christmas and I hope with all my heart your dad and I can make it a wonderful first Christmas for you. It's a time for family, and we are a family now.

I'm so glad you came into our lives, Bonnie. Bearing a new life is really the most magnificent miracle in this world, and I'll never forget the closeness I felt for you and your dad the moment you were born.

December, 29th, 1979
~Mummy

This morning, for the first time, you slept till 8:15 which was a real relief for me, seeing as 6:30 is your usual waking time. You still haven't got a tooth yet, but you're completely mobile now, except for walking on your own. You dance, sing, and clap your hands, you even run to me when your dad chases you. You don't like having a bath. I don't think you mind the water, but as soon as I start to wash you, you become scared and want to get out of the tub. Your doctor said you would have learning difficulties and react in strange ways to some things. But I think she's being ridiculous. You are just human. Like all of us. Being premature has nothing to do with anything.

For your first Christmas, you got a sing-songy telephone, a scooter, a lamp, a stuffed dog with a puppy, a couple of wooden chess boards (silly uncles), a Paddington Bear, a cup, bowl and saucer with Peter Rabbit on them, plastic stacking blocks and a music box.

You keep opening and closing the music box. And every time the tinkling begins and the ballerina starts to spin, you want to put her in your mouth. I had to take it away so you wouldn't break her. I think you will love the music box so much when you learn that you don't need to eat it. I'm sorry it made you cry when I took it away, but I know you will understand it was for the best.

I was hoping we would have a good first Christmas with you and we did, it was excellent. Our next one should be even better.

I love you sweetheart.

January 3rd, 1980
~Mummy

I forgot to mention that we are going to give you this book when you're older, but every time I write in it you want to chew it. I hate saying no to you but you want everything. It's not enough that you have most things. I also need to encourage John to write in it more. It was his idea. He started it. I wish he would follow through. At least with something that could one day be such a treasure for you.

January 4th, 1980
~Mummy

Today you received an early birthday present from Grandma and Grandpa Miller. A truck and a beautiful old wrist watch from your great grandmother. I'll keep it for you until you're old enough to take care of it. Also, this morning you got a second tooth, now you have two upper front teeth, my little bunny rabbit.

January 12th, 1980
~Mummy

Bonnie, today was your first birthday and your dad and I love you more and more every day. You do such beautiful things and you're always making us laugh because you're such a character. You are the best little dancer I've ever seen, you really adore music. I baked a cake for your birthday and your dad and I decorated it together. You're very special to both of us and we love you very much.
xoxoxoxoxoxoxoxoxoxoxoxoxoxoxoxo

May 10th, 1980
~Mummy

You've started to walk now and every day you go a little further with a bit more confidence. I can't stop watching you, it's just wonderful. John missed your first step. ~~He was late home from work. He made stupid excuses.~~ I know it gets hard for him sometimes. You are quite the handful. He's the one who keeps telling me that all you need is love. I wish he believed his own advice.

January 12th, 1981
~Mummy

Today is your second birthday. When we ask you how old you are, you answer, "two" with a curt nod. You say a lot of words, but no sentences as yet, but it won't be long, I'm sure. John and I got you a rocking horse for your birthday among other presents from your little crèche friends and your family.

But all you're interested in right now is the jar of buttons I have on my dresser. I was reluctant to let you play with them, but thankfully you've gotten over putting everything in your mouth now.

One day when John was sitting on the living room floor with you, you asked for them. He spread them all over the rug and you both sat there, cross-legged, for over an hour, playing with them and talking about who knows what. I kept walking past just to look at your face and you seemed so enthralled! When you both stood up, and I went in gather to them up and put them back in the jar, the buttons were sorted into colours. John is brilliant at teaching you things. And he has so much patience with you. I wish he'd managed to be that patient with me.

You are a happy and secure little thing, though John and I haven't been living together since last June. But then, you have a lot of people who love you very much.

December 28th, 1981
~Mummy

These are some events of the recent past Bonnie:

On May 16th, you, me and Ted went overseas to Germany. You were excited about going on a plane, but I'm afraid it was a bit much for you (and us). The whole time you were sick with a throat infection and your crying made everybody on the plane shoot us dirty looks.

We stayed in Munich for one day. There, you were very sick, but put up with our running around so well. The three of us decided to have a sleep in the afternoon after our long flight. Ted and I were so tired we left you to your own devices. You must have slept too, but when you woke up and we were still sleeping, you decided to wake Ted up by wetting on him—we couldn't stop laughing!

We went to Hof the next day. There we stayed with Gertie and Fritz, Ted's uncle and aunt. You became very close to them. You learned to use a toboggan in their fake backyard slope. You liked it a lot with Ted. I'm glad you like him. You also rode on a tricycle with us, which you loved too.

You really adored it there. You learned how to speak a little German and to understand a lot. What a shame you won't remember all the great things you experienced there, but remember one thing, everyone got to know you and love you and you had a great time.

We arrived back home with everyone waiting for us on November 12th. You didn't forget anyone. Daddy was there with Mary. Oh, and of course, Ted's brother too. This whole time you've been talking so well. You surprised everyone.

Well, you've had your 3rd Christmas. This time you had a much better idea about what was going on. You saw Father Christmas at the mall and sat on his lap. He asked you what you wanted for Christmas and you said you wanted green lebküchen!

You call the Christmas tree a "Father Christmas tree". You were so overwhelmed with all the presents you were showered with. But you still prefer the wrapping and the bows and ribbons to what is actually inside them. One of the presents you received was decorated with feathers. You can't stop stroking them. I'm not sure if it's my imagination, but the look on your face when you do so is rather melancholic, as if you're mourning the death of the bird it came from ... but I'm probably looking too much into it.

On the 24th we went to see Oma and Opa, Ted's parents, in Springvale. You never want to leave there. In Germany, the big day is Christmas Eve, so the family gave you your presents then. On Sunday, you had a lunch with your father and Mary, and then another Christmas lunch at Grandma and Grandpa Miller's in the afternoon. If only my parents were still alive to meet their beautiful grandchild.

Ted and I then picked you up to take you to Ted's brother's to play with his kids. You had a very busy Christmas day. You enjoyed every bit of the attention given to you. But it's funny, sometimes you go really quiet. Not a bad quiet. You have an odd expression of contentment on your face. I like to think you are just leisurely reflecting on your day.

I wish I could keep note of all the funny things you do and say. One thing I love is that you kiss whatever part of the body you can reach. Anything from bums, toes to armpits!

Merry Christmas, my darling Bonnie. I love you more each day. There is so much you give to all that know you, especially me.

December 29th, 1981
~Mummy

I just thought I'd write down some of my thoughts about you and my life with you.

Bonnie, I'm overawed when I think of the short time you have been alive. Barely three years. Yet I can't remember how life for me was before you, or how I ever lived before you came along.

I don't know how things will be for you when you realise what Mummy and Daddy mean. Your father loves you as I do, but so does Ted. He's not your real father, but he has done everything a father would. Especially love you. He gives you so much of it. It would be nice if one day you could call him Daddy instead of "my Ted." But I suppose that's my fault for introducing him as a friend in the beginning. I didn't really have much choice as I didn't know what I wanted then. But, one thing led to the other, and it just felt like the right thing to do. For you.

I will never forget what love with your father was like, you came from it and no one can regret that. We all love you so much. I know our decision not to live together might bring you hardships, but I hope my love for you may take away any doubts or confusion you might experience.

Bonnie, sometimes you make life hard for me. You throw lots of tantrums and you always want your own way.

Especially when it comes to sweets. You also have such clumsy moments and you hurt yourself. Today, you went to the toilet alone and the seat fell down on your nose. You've got quite a lump, tomorrow it will probably be a bruise. Poor thing. I think it hurts me more than it does you.

Most of the time though, my love, you're a well-behaved angel. I can take you anywhere and feel assured that you won't break things or make things difficult. You're mostly very sociable and good-natured. Although everyone says you have Ted's temper. Funny, they also say you have his nose! I don't bother telling them that he is your stepdad. It would just end up being a long and irrelevant conversation.

No matter what happens, I hope we can be friends when you grow up. I'll work very hard to make that happen because I always want you to feel secure in talking to me, trusting me and confiding in me.

I love you now and always!

Your Mum, Mama, Mummy, Ma, Penny.

January 7th, 1982
~Mummy

Today your Daddy and Mary have taken you for the after-noon. You were so happy to be going with them. When Mary is around you seem to have no need for me. You've become her shadow, and your poor mum is left on the side-lines. You change so much when you're around her. You become so defiant! You won't listen to me, talk to me or show me any affection. As far as you're concerned, I don't exist.

I suppose I should be grateful you have a half-sister. I've always thought about having another baby so you'd have someone to play with, but it scares me. I don't think I could cope.

This is the beginning of a change to our relationship, I think. No matter how much I would like to be your best friend, we are still mother and daughter, and that in itself seems to be a barrier. I wonder if you, (meaning us) can ever break through that. I will always feel too protective of you because you are part of me, and you, through this, will probably feel restricted and a bit overwhelmed by it.

I hope that someday you will understand that a mother who loves her child could never be blasé about its existence. The umbilical cord is physically severed, but not emotion-ally. That is, at least, as far as the mother is concerned. I used to take my mother for granted so much. Completely inconsiderate of her feelings. Only after having you did I realise how my mother must have felt with all the inconsideration I displayed. Taking love for granted. Mothers are human, I've found. We have the same needs as children. We all want, and more importantly, need to be cared about. People aren't disposable. We don't get thrown out no matter how many scars are left on us through our experiences. Physical or emotional.

Bonnie, for myself the emotional pains are always the most tragic to overcome. Because of my love for you, I know it will be extremely difficult to see you go through various growing pains, but I know that on the whole, you alone must work through them. Make your own mistakes and hopefully learn from them.

Bonnie, you will always have my trust! I hope you never abuse it. As you grow you will learn that trust will either make your life happy or sad. And I think you'll find that it's the people you love the most who will ultimately betray it. I don't understand why this is. You'd think it would be the opposite, wouldn't you? I suppose when you care about someone, the fear of hurting them must make us do silly things. Sometimes I find comfort in that fact. It seems to be the only thing keeping my chin up right now—the fact that your daddy still cares.

December 26th, 1982
~Mummy

Well, we've had Christmas now. You're not a baby anymore so you take in everything around you. I love to watch you so very much. I also love it when you say "I love you" a hundred times a day. I often wonder if you understand what it means.

You call me "my Ted", and Ted "Mummy" for fun. You're using your humour quite often now. One day, you brought me in some of those yellow flowers from the weeds in our back yard, and you asked me to put them in a vase. I said to you that they don't smell very nice, so you told me, "Don't smell them then. Just put them in a vase to look at." There's no arguing with you. You know exactly what you want and your reason and logic extends mine and Ted's by far.

Happy Christmas, Bonnie.

February 12th, 1984
~Mummy

It's been too long since I've made any entries into this book so I'll try to catch up a bit. You've been writing your name now for at least eighteen months. You are also making great efforts at reading.

Your bedroom has been renovated now for about six months and you spend a lot of time in there pretending to be and do all sorts of things. You've taken to playing around with a broomstick as if you were a witch about to take off with it! You hold it between your legs, gallop on the spot like a horse, and say, "up-up-and-away!" Not sure if you can make up your mind whether you want the broom to be a horse or not. Maybe you're just making it your own. A unicorn, perhaps?

Bonnie, you still love to dance, but now you are so much more dramatic in your movements and with such good rhythm too. You know all the songs that they show on TV Hits. I'm so proud of you, although we do have a lot of arguments and we don't often agree on things. I guess you've grown up so much, that it always takes my heart a while before it catches up to you.

February 13th, 1984
~Mummy

You had your first ballet lesson. You really enjoyed it. Ted and I sat and watched you. We didn't stop smiling all the way through. The hour passed quickly and you didn't want to stop. But then John came with Mary unexpectedly to pick you up and go for ice cream. I thought it was such a lovely surprise for you.

I'm sorry you had to see Ted lose his temper like that. Ted is just stressed with his fruit shop and he takes it out on everybody. It doesn't mean he hates your daddy. I promise. It's just that he had intended for us to spend the afternoon together. I didn't know he wasn't going back to the shop afterward.

Oh well. Men are funny creatures.

February 14th, 1984
~Mummy

A couple of weeks ago you started your first day of school. Only a few weeks after turning five years old. You have some new friends. Sara and Bianca. Sara has come here a few times to play with you. More and more I see how independent you are, as this morning. You walked so briskly and confidently into the school. I knew this marked the end of a wonderful time and the beginning of an even greater time for you.

My only hopes for you are to be as happy as you have been and that you never experience things too painfully like I do. I love you so very very much my darling, as do the others who make up your family. You are, and always will be, first and last in my thoughts and in my heart.

My biggest satisfaction is seeing you grow into a kind, gentle, intelligent, feeling, and compassionate person. Your beauty and talent, of course, are also wonderful bonuses. I hope one day you will understand the things I do and have done. When you love someone so much the instinct is to protect. I know I step over the line occasionally and for that I am truly sorry if it causes you pain or disillusion. We are all still learning.

February 15th, 1984
~Mummy

You're pretty lazy most of the time and that drives me berserk. You know how to read but you always refuse to. All you want most of the time is an ice cream or lollies and everything you do is related to those things in some way. You'll do anything for a lolly. John has been less involved with you lately. He needs to work things out a lot better with Mary.

You've been riding your bike a lot too. You were outside all day practising until you finally got it!

You've been patient with us as well. Ted's fruit shop takes up so much time some weeks, but you've always co-operated, and have never made it difficult for us. Those early mornings at the farmer's market are tough, I know. The other morning was quite entertaining though. You found a ladybug on an apple and squealed in delight so loudly that everybody around us went silent and smiled at your satisfaction. We stopped what we were doing for a little while so you could watch it crawl along your finger. Your eyes lit up and you said, "Look Mummy! The bug lady likes me!" and everyone around us chuckled. It was such a beautiful snapshot of time, I wish I'd had a camera.

I really should always have this book ready to write into because there is so much that we forget and if I wrote it all down those precious moments would be with us forever!

part two

love is a weapon

I LIFT UP MY Mickey Mouse skirt and pull down on the flicky-thread of my undies. But it squishes between my legs when I sit on the torlet seat.

It smells like a baby accident and a hospital in here and my heart goes all bumpy in my chest. I can smell that stinky liquid stuff that my mummy uses to make clothes white, and it always makes her rub her head after, and I have to bring her some Tic Tacs.

I can't tell any bodies I did this. I can't! They will all laugh at me and I don't like it when bodies laugh at me. When bodies laugh my belly goes all feeling not nice and tears comes out of my eyes. Mrs Haydon will come a-looking for me at *any* minute, wondering why I'm not back to get my school bag off my hook. The home-time bell just runged. I'm going to be in *so* much trouble. She's going to be *so* madly. Her googly eyes will go all wide through her yucky froggy glasses, and her cheeks will go so red that the chocolate splashes on her face will become not there. But the worsted thing will be when she sees what I done! She'll speak to me all funny. Like a witch. I bet she's a witch. Like in that book my Ted reads me where all the witches just look like normal mummies and daddies but have got wigs and they turn kids into mices. I hate that witch voice. Lots of teachers use that voice after they meet my mummy. Like they have ideas of making me into a dessert or sumfing.

Maybe I should flush my undies into the loo, and get wet hand towels to clean myself up without any grownups help. But I can't 'cause this stupid skirt is too short, and everyone will see my *chishy*. Mum showed my Ted her chishy. I sawed it too when I went to her bedroom in the middle of the night when I needed a glass of water and I couldn't reach the tap. I didn't go in. I don't want any bodies to do sumfing like that to my *chishy*. I can clean my own *chishy* now. I'm not a kitten.

Now everyone is leaving. They're running across the play-ground, making squeals, throwing balls against the torlet block wall. I can hear them voices. Those parents voices that sound like everything is rooly serious. My Ted speaks in that voice all the time. And when he does, my mummy does doll's eyes, and mumbles something about how my daddy was more fun and that she wishted he would come back. I don't think my Ted can hear when she says that. I wish my Ted and Daddy and Mary and Mummy and me could all just live together. I love all of them.

I can hear chains on the metal fence. It's Thursday. And there's no after-school care on Thursdays.

Oh *nose*, I'm going to get lockted in!

My yucky undies drop to the floor and the torlet door becomes a disgusting brown mess. I could do a finger painting in it, though. Should I lick it? Maybe it tastes like chocolate fudge. I know that sometimes things don't taste as badly like they smell. Sometimes my mummy cooks sumfing that's rooly stinky, but when I eat it, it's nice.

Should I yell for the caretaker to let me out? But how? How can I do that without him to saw this mess between my legs and all over the door?

My ears are hot. My heart goes bumpy. There are footsteps outside.

Clip. Clop. Clip. Clop. Clip. Clop!

They're at my door. I hold my breath tight and my face hurts. I stand still. Trying not to move or make noises. I can't speak. No *way*. I'd be founded out! But ... if I don't speak, I'll be lockted in here all the night. Who will bring my mummy her Tic Tacs if I'm lockted in here?

"Bonnie? Are you in there?" My breath comes in my neck rool quick. It's Mrs Haydon. She sounds funny. She sighs and makes a strange coughing. I think she's swallowing an orange pip by not-on-purpose.

Now I'm being founded out! I start to cry. I don't like crying. When I cry my mummy cries longer than me. And then my Ted gets all grumpy and drives off. And then Mummy whispers on the phone for ages.

I hold my hands in the air. The tears are falling over my face and making skin tickles.

"What's wrong?" It's Mrs Haydon again.

"Um," I suck my crying by mistake in my mouth. "I … pooed …"

Something weird happens in my head and my mouth goes all like a fish at the disgusting air around me. If my mummy was been here, she would gived me a paper bag to breathe into—I sawed her do it before—it maked her calmed. It would go out and in and make a cool crunching sound. It's fun to watch it, chooally. Her face changes shape. It looks like if she didn't get the air from inside the bag, she might just drop dead on the floor like a squished mouse that got squished in the laundry the other day.

"Oh, Bonnie, don't worry." That's Mrs Haydon again. "Look, stay put, and I'll go to the lost property box to find you a fresh pair of pants, okay?" Her voice goes all boomer-angy. Maybe I'm in Doctor Who's elevator, and if I just push the flush button I can make myself not here.

I won't be maded embarrassed. No bodies has to be told—just me and Mrs Haydon's secret. Maybe she's a good witch. I think she's putting a nice spell on me to make me feel safe. I take a deep sigh. Mrs Haydon leaves. I bend over like I'm going to spew but nothing comes out and it feels like Mr Stomach is doing some ballet in my tummy.

Mrs Haydon comes rushing back rool quick.

"Oh, Bonnie, darling, there's a woman here to pick you up."

Everything in the torlet goes on pause.

I look at the roof, wondering who it could be. Maybe it's Mary. She's never comed to pick me up before.

"I thought you said Mummy was walking you home today, Bonnie." That's Mrs Haydon again. She sounds worried.

"Is it Mary?" That's me asking, not Mrs Haydon. I feel much better now. It must be her. I love Mary. She's not as old as my mummy, but she's not young like me either. I think she's somewhere in the middle. It's fun because sometimes she plays stuff that I like. But sometimes she gets weird and tries to act like a grownup in front of my daddy. I play on my own when that happens. She wears bright red lipstick a lot and has frizzy yellow hair. She is a bit fat and squishy and smells like musk sticks. I like her hugs.

I heard Mummy saying to Daddy one day that when people sawed her and Mary together in the street, that lesbians would try to pick them up. I'm glad Mummy likes Mary. But why did that made my Ted go all upset? And where were the bodies going to take them? Did they have a blue Ute like my Ted? Maybe I should get Mummy to tell *me* the story. My Ted's always in a hurry, and he sometimes drives too fast. But sometimes it's fun. I like to lie on my back in the back bit of the Ute and look at the clouds and think that I'm in an airplane without any roof.

"The lady says that Mummy got held up at the fruit shop. Does that sound right to you?" That's Mrs Haydon again. She does a funny hiccup.

I think she hearded me nod.

"Okay, then. I'll go look for some clean pants and then I'll collect your things and take you to her, okay?" She waits a second for me to say sumfing. I can hear her turn on her foot and wait like the pause button makes bodies wait in the VCR.

"Okay," I whisper, feeling Mr Stomach doing dances. I think Mary picking me up means that I don't have to go home and watch my mummy pretend she hasn't been crying all alone in the kitchen, while my Ted lockted himself in his study room pretending to be smart.

Sometimes my Ted takes me to the fruit shop, and he buys me stuffed potatoes for dinner and Violet Crumble for dessert. But it gets boring sometimes. Mummy and my Ted look at me through the silent glass window of the office, with stupid smiles. I know they just want to make sure I don't go make holes in the chopped up watermelon pieces. I did it a few times. My Ted yelleded rool loud.

Mrs Haydon comes back. I unlock the door, my legs going all shaking from the feelings. She has a pair of blue undies with robots on them. Boy knickers. *Eew!* She nods at the floor. I lift my feet out of the holes, making hard to not tumble over.

Mrs Haydon helps me get cleaned up. She washes my undies in the sink, making sure she doesn't touch my stuff, then dries them under the electric hand machine and puts them into a plastic bag for me to take back home.

"Here you are, Bonnie. Good as gold." She gives me the plastic bag, opens my school bag and moves her head to say invisible words. I think she wants me to put it inside the bag. But I don't want to keep them. If I keep the undies, I have to tell Mummy what I done. But I can't tell Mummy what I done because I have to be a grownup. I have to be able to take care of myself. Soon Mummy won't be able to take care of me anymore. I sawed her once, come home, and speak funny, and then fall over and go to sleep. She was still there when I gotted up in the morning. There was wet stuff on the floor next to her bed and it smelled like fish fingers.

I just spewded up in my bag.

"Oh dear." That's Mrs Haydon again. She stands up and wipes her forehead with some paper towel. "You must have a stomach bug, my dear. Your accident couldn't have been helped, I'm sure. Let's get this cleaned up and you safely home to bed. Hmm? The lady outside will make sure you get home to bed? Won't she?"

I nod. Maybe my mummy will sit with me now, instead of hiding in her room and writing in that book. Most of the time she just looks at that book and cries. But last night she wrote in it for ages and gave it some flowers.

Tape #01

Dr Wright: Mummy tells me that you miss Daddy. Do you want to talk about it?
Bonnie: *[scribbles on paper with green crayon]*
Dr Wright: She says you're always asking for him and getting upset.
Bonnie: *[nods]*
Dr Wright: She also says you visit him a lot. Is that right?
Bonnie: *[nods]*
Dr Wright: You know that Mummy does everything she can for you to see him. She loves you very much. Would you like to tell me why you get so upset?
Bonnie: My daddy buys me lots of I-screams.
Dr Wright: Does Mummy not allow you to eat ice cream?
Bonnie: *[shakes head]* It doesn't make logic.
Dr Wright: What doesn't make sense, Bonnie?
Bonnie: It's silly. No bodies scream when they eat I-screams. They should be called I-quiets.
Dr Wright: *[laughs]* Would you like to explain that further?

Bonnie: *[blank stare, continues to draw in green]*

Dr Wright: How come you don't like any of the other colours, Bonnie?

Bonnie: Daddy said green is a colour of being safe.

Dr Wright: Do you believe that too?

Bonnie: *[nods]*

Dr Wright: Why do you think green means safe?

Bonnie: *[shrugs]*

Dr Wright: You have a logical reason for everything, Bonnie. I'd like to hear it.

Bonnie: No thanks.

Dr Wright: I'm a little bit confused. How come you don't like eating the green jellybeans?

Bonnie: *[stops scribbling, looks up and offers a blank stare]*

Dr Wright: Have you had enough talking today, Bonnie?

Bonnie: *[nods]* I don't eat the green ones because they taste like medicine.

February 16th, 1984
~Mummy

I sent Mary to pick you up from school today. The guilt is killing me, but I just didn't know what else to do. I hope you forgive me for writing horrible things in this book, but you must know the truth. I don't know how long I'll wait until I give this book to you. Maybe when you start high school, maybe university, maybe I'll wait until you have kids of your own. Whenever it is, I want you to know that I'm sorry. I miss your father, and Ted, though a good provider, is getting grumpier and grumpier. The shop isn't doing very well and today he asked me to send you to live with your dad and Mary for a while until we get back on our feet! Can you believe this? I would never ever ever send you away! I hope you know that. You are the only thing in this world that I would gladly starve for.

I have to tell you, I cry a lot. I try not to. I'm not sure why I feel so unhappy. Maybe I miss John. Maybe I'm sad that I never did anything with my life, besides have you, that I can be proud of. I'm so glad you haven't seen me cry. I can't even begin to imagine how that would make you feel. I still haven't decided whether I should have Ted collect you from your dad's when he closes the shop, or just let you stay there overnight. I know you love Mary and you'll probably have fun. But I fear, being the only other constant female influence in your life, that you'll end up loving her more than me.

John still hasn't written in this book since you were born. I keep offering it to him, but he keeps refusing. I'm not going to ask anymore. I'm tired of it. Honestly, I think he's scared of all the feelings in here. But I do secretly hope he reads it all again. Maybe it will help us have a better relationship. I hate to admit it, but I would take him back in a heartbeat. Maybe I should just let you stay overnight and insist John bring you back tomorrow. Maybe the more we see each other, the more chance there is of rekindling what brought us together in the first place.

Wait. The phone is ringing ...

I just got a call from your dad. He said you have a terrible stomach bug and that he'll bring you back tomorrow afternoon.

Perhaps it's fate.

PS: I've started pressing some flowers for you. You were so fascinated by Grandma Miller's collection that I thought we should start our own! So far I've got some jasmine, daisies, and buttercups pressed between the pages of this book.

I DIDN'T GO TO school today so I get to play a shop with Mary all day while Daddy is at work. I don't rooly understand what he does. But he always is talking about numbers in shapes and the sky, and always is leaving the house wearing the same boring old thing.

Anyway, how the shop game works is that I pull all the medicine bottles out of the bathroom cupboard, and I spread them all pretty on the kitchen counter. Every two minutes, Mary comes in and tells me that she's not feeling good. So I ask her to splain me how she feels so I can sell her the right bottle. It's not good to make mistakes with sick bodies because if you do they might be getting sicker.

Most of the time, I don't really understand the words she says, but I think they're called SimTims. But that just makes me want Tim Tams, so I just give her a packet of aspirin to take the pain away and ask her to go to the milk bar to buy me some. She's good like that. She doesn't get those silly lines in her face every time I ask for sweets. She just goes and gets them. It's really simple. I think she should tell my mummy how simple it is.

After a while of playing, Mary gets bored and speaks on the phone. She always twirls the cord around her finger and gets her whole body wrapped up in it. It's silly. Sometimes I don't think she's really a grownup. Maybe she's just playing dress-ups.

Daddy walks in with a big smile on his face, and Mary skips up to him like a little girl and gives him a kiss on the cheek.

"Did you go to see your mother today?" That's Daddy speaking to Mary, not me. She nods and does doll's eyes and hangs her head to the side making a stupid groaning sound. She sounds like my Ted in the mornings.

"I still don't understand why I should go, Dad. She can't remember me."

"It's just good to keep touching base."

I don't know what sports has to do with what they are saying but it sounds serious. It always sounds serious with grownups.

"The doctor did say she might get her memory back at any time, remember? And by seeing you on a frequent basis can trigger flashbacks. Please just keep going to visit her."

"But it's been years! You're not going to send me back to live with her are you?"

Daddy's head goes all wobbly in his hands. He hasn't come to say hello to me yet. That happens a lot when he speaks to Mary. Chooally, it happens to all bodies when they speak to Mary. I don't understand why. Will I be that special when I get bigger?

"Sweetheart …"

Daddy looks over at me and smiles.

"Are you feeling any better?" That's Daddy speaking to me now, not Mary. I nod and eat another Tim Tam. I don't know why he bovvers to smile when the smile is really invisible sad words. Now Mary looks at me too and does doll's eyes again. That makes my Mr Stomach feel like there are fuzzy clouds in it. I don't think it was a nice thing to do to me. Sometimes I think grownups are stupid just pretending to be smart.

Mary punches Daddy in the shoulder, and he looks at her funny. Those looks send feelings *all* through the room. Like the air is going hard in our nostrils. Daddy moves his head towards me and Mary makes an annoying sound with her tongue. There they are again. Those invisible words. Why don't they just say them out loud? It would be so much easier to understand.

Daddy walks out and Mary takes the Tim Tams away from me. I want to tell her not to, but my mouth is full of one, and Mummy tolded me it's rude to open my mouth when there's food in it.

Mary grabs a tea towel and wipes it across my mouth. It hurts and I say *ow*, but it doesn't rooly sound like *ow* because I have a tea towel over my mouth.

"Stop being a baby." That's Mary speaking, not me.

"I'm not being a baby, you're too violent."

"Violent? Where did you learn a word like violent?"

"None of your beeswax. I go to school."

Mary throws the tea towel on the counter and lifts me off the tall stool because I'm too short for the tall stool. I don't like being short. If I was tall like Mummy and Daddy I could poke my chin on the top of Mary's head. And then when she is pretending to be a grownup, I would be pointing my finger at her, and saying to her, "Don't misbehave, young lady," and make her go to her bedroom without any dessert.

Mary laughs and makes an annoying sound through her nose and she sounds like sumfing off the Animal Farm show on Channel 2. I don't know why Daddy only watches Channel 2. I hearded him say to Mary that all the other channels are full of shit. Shit is a bad word. I askted Mary what shit means and she tolded me that it means poo. So that makes me think and I think that it doesn't make logic for TV channels to be full of poo. Only torlets and undies can be full of poo. I didn't say that to Mary because I didn't want her to be in trouble with Daddy for telling me about a bad word.

"Go get cleaned up for dinner." That's Mary telling me to get cleaned up for dinner.

"But I'm not hungry." That's me not Mary.

"That's because you ate half a packet of Tim Tams!"

"That's because you gave them to me."

"Well I thought you were only going to eat *one*."

"But you didn't tell me to only eat one."

"Why do I need to tell you to only eat one? You know it's almost dinner time."

"When Mummy gives me sweets, she always tells me how much I can have."

"But I'm not your mother."

"But you're a grownup and you should know better, young lady." That was me talking, not Mary, and I used "young lady" a lot better than my Ted because Mary really is a young lady.

Mary puts her hands on her hips and her mouth goes all thin. She walks out of the room and calls for Daddy. She comes back in with him and they stand at the kitchen door staring at me with googly eyes and my Daddy has a funny smile on his face, but it's another smile that doesn't mean he's happy, I think he's got feelings of being annoyed, but I think he's annoyed with Mary, not me.

He's changded clothes. He's wearing a tracksuit now. Mary says sumfing to him all quiet and he mumbles sumfing back all angry man, but trying not to be angry man.

"Honey, how is your stomach after all those biscuits? Are you feeling okay? Do you want an antacid?"

I was feeling okay until he said that I should be eating one of those disgusting lollies, they taste like disgusting chalk and make me want to chuck.

Then he comes up to me and rubs my back all nice, but then I can hear my Mr Stomach do dancing again and I chuck up *awwwl* over his feet.

February 17th, 1984
~Mummy

John just called to say he's on his way home with you. Apparently Mary fed you a box of Tim Tams. Silly girl. She may be smart enough to be accepted into medicine at a prestigious university, but she certainly needs to learn a bit of common sense.

John also told me that you had a bit of a fight with her. Can I say I'm secretly satisfied with that outcome? I know it's horribly selfish of me. But I've been so distant lately, and I often wonder how it's affecting you. It can't be easy seeing Ted and I argue about you all the time. I know that all he wants is the best for you. For us. But in my opinion, the best thing for a little girl is to be with her mother, regardless of her financial situation.

Can I make a confession? I'm not sure I love Ted as much as I used to. I thought I did. But I think I only married him so that you could have a decent upbringing. Your father has enough of his own problems to deal with so I couldn't possibly ask him to support you after everything that happened with his ex-girlfriend and daughter. I feel sorry for Mary, I really do. But I am just a bit jealous of her. Trying to accept that I wasn't his first love was hard enough, but to find out he had another daughter who needed him was just horrible. I could never wish anybody to experience such a thing. But life is funny like that. One minute you *have everything you want and need and love. The next, the whole world is turning upside down and you're giving everything you love away.*

Oops! There's the doorbell ...

Tape #02

Dr Wright: What do you think of Mary?
Bonnie: She's pretty.
Dr Wright: Do you like being around her?
Bonnie: *[nods]* Sometimes. *[picks at wood on edge of table]*
Dr Wright: Why only sometimes?
Bonnie: *[stares blankly, opens mouth slightly, shrugs]*
Dr Wright: It's okay, you can talk to me.
Bonnie: *[takes an exaggerated deep breath then breathes out with cheeks puffed up]*
Dr Wright: *[waits patiently]*
Bonnie: Daddy does invisible words with her.
Dr Wright: Invisible words?
Bonnie: *[nods]*
Dr Wright: What are invisible words?
Bonnie: Mary is more special. Mary is a grownup.
Dr Wright: Do you think she's more special than you?
Bonnie: *[shrugs, nods]*
Dr Wright: Bonnie, sometimes grownups don't understand that their actions

look like something different to what they really are. Daddy just speaks differently with Mary because she's a bit bigger than you. It doesn't mean he loves her more. All parents love their children equally. You understand?

Bonnie: *[shrugs, nods, picks at edge of table]*

Dr Wright: Do you want to play a game?

Bonnie: *[looks at Dr Wright, nods, smiles]*

Dr Wright: What would you like to do. It's your choice.

Bonnie: Can we play the shop like I do with Mary? I like to give medicine.

Dr Wright: Do you want to be a doctor when you grow up?

Bonnie: No, I want to give medicine from a shop with a green cross.

Mummy opens the door and she's holding the book and she has a pen between her teeth. She smiles at me and takes the pen out of her teeth and puts it behind her ear. Then she smiles at Daddy. But the smile is different than the one she gave to me.

Daddy rests his hand on my shoulder and pushes me forward a bit. I think that means I should be going inside. Again with the invisible words. I go in and watch from behind Mummy's legs, but not touching.

The sun is getting tired because the light is going away, but it's still shining some happy thoughts behind Daddy's head. It's pretty, and I want to visit the sun one day, like those men on TV did visit the moon. I think they should have beened to the sun. Then they wouldn't be needing those big stupid suits to keep them warm.

Mummy winks and blows me a kiss and then speaks to Daddy all softly. She holds the book to her chest like she's hugging it. Daddy touches it but it looks like Mummy is holding it more tight. She has that smile full of sad words, and she steps backwards a bit.

"You had your chance. I'm over it." That was Mummy all low and whispery a bit angry woman sounding.

"I wasn't ready before. But I'm ready now."

"Why now? What's changed?" Mummy leans her

shoulder against the inside of the door and Daddy puts
his hands in his pockets and looks at Mummy's feet. He
looks at her feet a lot. I think he always is thinking that she
should buy some new shoes because she always is wearing
the same ones.

"I'm not sure. Maybe the guilt of leaving you is catching
up to me." Daddy said that last bit rool quiet still looking
at Mummy's shoes. I don't know what guilt means but it
sounds pretty and a bit like gold.

They go on pause and Mummy sniffs and rubs her nose.

"Ted will be home soon." That was Mummy, not Daddy.

"Can I have the book?"

"Not tonight."

"Why not?"

"I haven't finished with it. I was in the middle of an entry
when you arrived."

I don't think she's talking about the same entry as I know.
But I don't think doors can fit in that book. Unless they are
magic doors. Maybe they are doors that gobble up bodies.
Maybe there's demons in it. Maybe it's full of badly and
that's why Mummy cries at it.

"What if I come back tomorrow and collect it?"

Mummy moves her head. I can't see if she's saying yes or
no in those grownup invisible words. Then she closes the
door in Daddy's face without saying goodbye. I think that's
rude.

Mummy turns around and looks to me. She gives me
one of those smiles. The ones where she wants me to think

she's happy but she's really not. She puts her pen and book on the coffee table and gets down on her knees to hug me. She's warm and she smells like those swirlded black things that you can get at the milk bar. They come in red too. And there's also a funny plant in the backyard that smells like the black swirlded stuff too. Sometimes I chew on it but then I spit it out because the taste goes away and it goes all like soggy grass.

I wish I could go into *Alice in Wonderland*. Then I could eat that cake because I like cake, but this cake could make me go big, and then I would pick up Mummy and Daddy and put them in a box like hamsters and keep them in my bedroom forever.

"Why does Daddy want the book?" That's me asking, not Mummy.

Mummy breathes rool loud through her nostrils and it sounds like she's sniffing in caramel fudge. She holds me outward and makes her lips do that pressing together thing.

"It's not important, pumpkin."

"It *is* important." That's me and I stamp my foot.

Mummy smiles like she thinks she knows more than me. Grownups do that a lot. They think they know more than me. They don't know more than me, I know it.

Mummy makes a little piglet noise, "Why is it important?"

"It has to be! You're always holding it, and writing in it, and ..."

I turn my head and look at the book on the table. I

pobably shouldn't say it. Maybe it will make her madly and she won't let me have dessert tomorrow.

"And what sweetie?"

"I don't know. I just think it's an important book. If Daddy wants it like you do, it must be important. What's in it? Is it full of sadness and that's why he wants to take it away?"

Mummy laughs and it makes me feel stupid. But I'm not stupid. I know that there is something in that book that keeps making her cry. When she gives it to Daddy, I have to tell him not to ever give it back.

February 17th, 1984 cont.
~Mummy

… I gave you some chicken noodle soup. It made you sleepy right away and I've just put you to bed. I'm a little surprised at your fascination with this book. You've never showed interest in it before. Am I a bad mother for not noticing? If you keep seeing me with the book, I can't even begin to imagine what other things you've seen. Oh my goodness. I'm so sorry!

I could just tell you about it, but I know you. You'll want me to read you the entries straight away. You'll want details, you'll ask questions I'm not ready to answer, and I'll give you answers you won't understand. So, sweet Bonnie, you're going to have to wait. It's going to have to remain between me and John for a few more years yet.

I am really confused about why he's asking for the book now, though. Just when I was ready to stop pushing him to write in it. I was all prepared, and now he's thrown me for a sixer. I wish I could ask you if you've noticed anything different about him when you stay there. Has he met anyone else yet? Do you think he's still in love with me? Do you think he'll read all my entries before he starts writing his own?

Do you think … it might bring him back?

I WAKE UP IN my own bed, and it's still dark. The moon has that face on it again. Mummy keeps telling me there is a man on it, but I think that's silly. If there was a man on it, his head wouldn't be as big as the whole planet! I think they are mountains and lakes and rivers and trees and big holes from fire balls in space. Daddy tolded that to me.

I think he knows more than my mummy. Because my mummy doesn't have a job. She stays in the house all day so I'm not alone when I comed home from school. My daddy goes out every day and comes back and talks about things I don't understand. Daddy's job is even better than my Ted's. My Ted's job is just full of fruit. Even *I* can remember the different colours of them all. As Mummy says, it's not rocket science. I guess she's smart with sumf-ings. She knows when bodies are smart and when bodies are just pretending to be smart. Daddy is smart. And I think Mummy knows that my Ted is just pretending to be smart. That's why she always is doing doll's eyes when he's not looking and learning about money in his study room.

I can hear my Ted's voice in the kitchen. Plates and stuff are making sounds that Mummy says will wake me up. I know that, because sometimes, when she lets me fall asleep in her lap on the couch, my Ted goes into the kitchen and moves stuff around. It's always late and she does a shooshing and tells him that he'll wake me up. But I'm already awake. I just have my eyes closed. I like listening to stuff that no-one knows I can hear. Because it's when some of the grownup invisible words stop hiding.

Mummy does a mumble-mumble.

My Ted does a mumble a bit louder.

Mummy does a longer mumble-mumble.

"No, I've had *enough* of this." That was my Ted. Yelling rool loud.

Then my mummy goes "Shoosh, you'll wake up Bonnie."

Then my Ted goes, "It's always about Bonnie and this ... this *damn* book! When are you going to stop farting about in that book and do some real paperwork? Help the business for God's sake. Help *us*." Then I hear a big boom! and I hear sumfings going clatter-bang. I don't think my Ted understands my mummy sometimes. Because I've never seen her fart in the book. I think that was a silly thing to say, and if my daddy was here he would tell my Ted to get his facts straight before making a kyousations. I don't know what a kyousations is, but I know that if Daddy said that to my Ted that he would stop making not nice music with the kitchen things.

"And what if I don't *want* to help us?" That was Mummy talking. She yelled rool loud and she doesn't do that much. My heart goes bumpy in my chest a bit because Mummy doesn't sound like Mummy when she uses her angry voice.

Sumfing crashes and smashes and goes clangety-clang bang and Mummy does a squealing and starts to cry rool loud, almost as loud as her angry voice. My heart goes bumpy rool fast now and I jump rool fast out of bed and run to the kitchen. My mummy is kneeling on the floor crying with her arms over her head and my Ted kicks her side and she tumbles over and rolls up like a baby. Her body is shaking like mine felt like it was shaking in the loo when I pooed in my undies.

My Ted looks up and wipes his hand over his mouth like he is getting rid of chocolate smudges from Tim Tams and says sumfing in a rool low voice and steps closer to me. He's got the book in his hand. But my Ted is making me scared playing dress-ups like a monster and I run to my room and cry into my pillow and under my banket.

There must be monsters in the book that make my Ted to be mean. I'm surely of it. Tomorrow morning I'm going to be burying the book in the backyard.

The book has demons and has to go to the devil to get a smack.

Tape #03

Dr Wright: Ted brought you in today. Do you like it when Ted drives you here to see me?
Bonnie: *[nods]*
Dr Wright: Do you have as much fun with Ted as you do with Daddy?
Bonnie: *[nods]*
Dr Wright: Tell me about some fun stuff you do with Ted.
Bonnie: Why?
Dr Wright: Because I'm interested.
Bonnie: Why?
Dr Wright: I like it when you tell me stories. You're a great storyteller. Did you know that?
Bonnie: *[smiles, nods]*
Dr Wright: Excellent. So can you tell me one of your brilliant stories?
Bonnie: *[nods, twists hands between knees and stretches arms]* Once upon a time, there was a man named my Ted. *[looks at Dr Wright for approval]*
Dr Wright: Good. Go on, Bonnie. I'm listening.
Bonnie: Well ... he likes to be playing with a coloured box that moves bits and pieces to put all the colours on one side.
Dr Wright: A Rubik's cube?

Bonnie: *[nods]*

Dr Wright: Did he teach you how to use it?

Bonnie: Stop trupting, I haven't finished the story!

Dr Wright: Sorry, go on.

Bonnie: *[shifts in seat, pushes hair from forehead]* Well, my Ted isn't very smart because I tolded him to fix it so all the greens could be on the same side and he sat with me on the flying carpet, and I made us go up in the air, so there could be magic around us, so he could fix it for all the greens to be on the same side.

Dr Wright: Wow, Bonnie. So did Ted manage to get all the greens on the same side?

Bonnie: *[shakes her head]*

Dr Wright: Oh, that's a shame. Did you ask your Mummy to have a go?

Bonnie: *[shakes her head]* No, but I did it.

Dr Wright: You did it?

Bonnie: *[nods head and smiles widely, squashes hands between her knees]* Why do you ask tricky questions like all the grownups?

Dr Wright: My question isn't tricky, Bonnie. Why do you think it's tricky?

Bonnie: You ask a question but you

already got my answer. My Ted asks tricky questions. I think they're silly. I think grownups are more silly than silly girls.

Dr Wright: *[laughs]* So, are you sure you got all the colours on one side?

Bonnie: Yes! I'm smart! I know much much much much more than my Ted.

Dr Wright: *[smiles]* Of course you're smart, Bonnie, we all know how special you are, and how fast you are learning. You have been making great progress.

Bonnie: *[nods and looks out the window]*

Dr Wright: So when you showed Ted that you fixed it, what did he say? Was he surprised?

Bonnie: *[nods and giggles]* He said, *[deepens voice]* you are the mostest intelligent girl on this planet, young lady. *[giggles and falls backward into couch]*

Dr Wright: Wow, that's fantastic. It must make you feel good when Ted says such nice things to you, huh?

Bonnie: *[nods]* But it doesn't make logic.

Dr Wright: What doesn't make sense, Bonnie?

Bonnie: I'm not a young lady, I'm just a girl.

IT'S ROOL EARLY IN the morning I think. And the moon is still up, but it's a bit light blue outside. That's another reason why I don't think the man on the moon makes logic. If he did make logic, he would be making himself go sleepy when the sun comed up. Because that would be the polite thing to do.

Mummy comes into my room and sits on the edge of my bed. She does that shooshing again, but a bit quieter, like she's taking orders from herself.

"Sweetie, are you okay?"

I nod.

My banket makes a noise around my ears because I have it pulled right up to my nose.

"I'm sorry about before. Ted loses his temper sometimes, but it's because he's working hard to support us. You understand that, don't you?" I nod again, but she's got it all wrong. I know Daddy is the smart one, but I always thoughted my mummy was smarter than me. How can she not see that it's the book that's doing the badly?

"Have you got in-some-knee-ah?" That's me asking mummy, not her asking me. Sometimes she gets this thing called in-some-knee-ah and it means she can't sleep poperly. She makes me bring her Tic Tacs for that too, but I think they're another kind of Tic Tac because they look a bit bigger.

I think the body who invented English wasn't very smart. I don't understand how the poblem is in the knee. My Daddy said that when we go to sleep, that our brains are having a nap. So that means it has sumfing to do with the head. It should be called in-some-head-ah. I think the *ah* is like the *ow*. That makes logic because when you don't get much sleep the brain hurts. I know that because Mummy rubs her head like she does when she cleans.

Mummy shakes her head. That means no. In some other country it means yes. I learnted that in school.

"Can you keep a secret?"

I nod again. Sometimes I like secrets. Specially the ones when Daddy says he's got a surprise and takes me to the zoo, or to the spinning pool, or to the Victoria Market for hot jam doughnuts. Grownups like secrets too. I think they like them more than kids sometimes.

"I'm taking something to your dad. It's a surprise. Ted doesn't have to go to the farmer's market this morning, so he's sleeping in. Can you do me a favour, sweetie?"

I nod and I hope I don't have to be raking the leaves with the shaker stick again. The shaker stick is too heavy and the leaves run away from the mountains I make and I have to rake them with the shaker stick too many times.

"Can you be really quiet this morning so you don't wake up Ted?"

"What about brekkie?"

"You know how to fix yourself some cereal, sweetie. Ted really needs the rest. He works too hard and he's exhausted."

I look out the window at the sunshine saying hello. It's getting much lighter and some birds are going twit-twit-twit. I think it's the sparrows. I wish I could hold a sparrow. They are cute. And sometimes I like to make up little stories about them. Like how they turn little kids into pretty songs and they live forever.

"Honey? Can you do that for me?" That's mummy. She is still all whisperly but more loud whisperly.

Mummy rubs my knees through the banket. I nod again, and she smiles as if she's not worried anymore. Then she tip toes away and blows me a kiss at the door. It squeaks a bit when she closes it. But she doesn't close it all the way. She leaves a gap for the monsters to find a way out in the middle of the night. But the night is over. It was pobably just an in-a-cent mistake. My Ted says Mummy makes those types of mistakes a lot. But I don't understand how a mistake can live inside a money coin.

I think Mummy is silly for asking me not to wake up my Ted. Grownups always ask questions when they chooally really want to give you an order. Mummy says it's polite to ask. But I think asking is like lying sometimes. It's just like a trick. And I think tricks like that are a bit mean. My Ted plays tricks on Mummy all the time. They're a bit more serious than the trick Mummy just played on me, though. My Ted asks her questions and then doesn't even let Mummy answer. He answers them for her! Why does he even bovver asking if he is going to tell her how to answer him? That's a mean trick. But now I'm thinking that it's the book's badly. It's the book's badly that makes my Ted go violent and ask tricky questions. When my daddy asks me questions, they're not tricky. They are real. And if I answer them in a way he doesn't like, most of the time it's okay, and we do sumfing that we both like to be doing. I love my daddy. I know I don't really know what love looks like, but I think it's my feelings.

My daddy is nicer than my Ted. I think he's smarter too. But my Ted is still nice, just not as nice as Daddy.

Tape #04

Dr Wright: Daddy tells me you're fasci-nated with the stars. Do you think you'd like to become an astrophysicist like him one day?

Bonnie: *[frowns]* Pardon?

Dr Wright: An astrophysicist. That's what your Daddy is. He tells me you enjoy looking at the sky at night. Is that true?

Bonnie: *[nods]* I like to be looking at the moon.

Dr Wright: Only the moon?

Bonnie: *[shakes head]*

Dr Wright: What else do you like to look at?

Bonnie: The man.

Dr Wright: Do you mean God?

Bonnie: *[frowns]* Pardon?

Dr Wright: Some people believe God made the earth and everything on it, including us. Is that who you mean by the man?

Bonnie: *[shakes head]* I mean the man that Mummy likes to be looking at.

Dr Wright: *[frowns, swallows]* Bonnie, can you tell me about the other man in Mummy's life?

Bonnie: Mummy says he looks down on us from the moon, and keeps the moon safe from purple monsters.

Dr Wright: *[sighs with relief, smiles]* Ah, I see. You're talking about the man on the moon! He's an interesting fellow, isn't he?

Bonnie: *[shakes head]* He's not real. Mummy thinks he's real, but she's wrong.

Dr Wright: Oh? Why do you think that?

Bonnie: She's being silly.

Dr Wright: Why?

Bonnie: I said, because he's not real!

Dr Wright: Bonnie, there's no need to shout. We're just having a conversation.

Bonnie: I don't want to have a conversation. I want to go home! *[crosses arms and frowns]*

Dr Wright: You can go home soon. We just need to finish up here first. Is that okay?

Bonnie: No! *[throws crayons at Dr Wright's face]*

Dr Wright: Bonnie, you shouldn't throw things at people. It's not nice. Would you like me to throw things at you?

Bonnie: *[huffs and shakes her head]*

Dr Wright: Okay ... let's continue ...

February 18th, 1984
~Daddy

I just read the first two entries in this book. My entries. I haven't lived up to anything I promised you, my love. I wish there was more I could do for you. But Penny doesn't want to intrude on my life. I guess that's my fault. I pushed you both away when I had to take custody of Mary and life got too hard.

I've matured a lot in five years, I believe. If only I was half the man I am now then, maybe I wouldn't have panicked about my new responsibilities, and we could have become one big family. One day I'll explain it all to you in detail, but simply put, Penny and I fought, a lot, and silly me thought it meant our marriage was over, and when my ex-girlfriend had that horrible accident, and I had to take care of Mary, I used it as an excuse to get out of the marriage. I regret it. I do. I now realise that those fights just meant we cared deeply for each other. What a fool I was. I hope one day you and your mother can forgive me.

But this book is meant to bring you joy, so enough writing about the hardships. Penny asked me not to read her entries. And she agreed not to read mine either. We will honour that. For you. The last thing we want is for our feelings to get in the way of this precious gift. This is for you, Bonnie. You only.

I'm sure Penny thinks this book was my idea. But really, it was hers. When you were about thirty-two weeks in gestation, she said to me, one hand on her belly, the other on my cheek, "If only there was a way to merge our hearts." I never told her that was the reason I bought you this book. I wish I had. I can't tell her now. It won't have the same meaning. And I think it will just make her sad. It seems she has enough of that already. I can see it in the lines around her eyes. Oh, how often I hope she is doing well and doesn't succumb to the tears. She is very sensitive, your mother. The smallest heartache triggers the waterworks. It used to make me angry. But now I understand that she can't help it. She is who she is. No one can change that. And who would want to?

Listen to me ramble on and on. It's one quality that is great at my workplace when we get into exciting discussions about the temperamental universe, but I'm afraid rambling on about things that don't make sense to you seems useless here.

Has anyone ever told you that actions speak louder than words? It's the best cliché in the book. And one that holds relevance in every possible life situation. Remarkable really that I believe such things, and then I write in a journal!

But Penny is right. We should continue to write in it. At least during the early years. I think it will be a nice thing to remember us by. And I like to believe that it may just grant us immortality. Just like the stars I love and cherish as much as you, Bonnie.

Penny and I have decided to drop this book off at each other's houses every couple of days. It will be a nice excuse to see more of her. More of you. She caught me by surprise this morning when she came by. I didn't think she was going to agree, but something must have happened at home last night for her to change her mind. She had a sparkle in her eye. One I haven't seen in years. I would have liked it if that sparkle were for me, but I think it's for you. It's her pride for you. Without you, I fear she'd have no sense of purpose and do something she'd regret.

But we can't have everything in this life. This is another lesson you will one day become familiar with. And I dug my own grave it seems. I suppose I should stop explaining what all these phrases mean because when you read this book you will probably be as old as me!

Just for the record, Penny was my only true love. There will never be another Penny for me. In fact, I don't think I ever want one. Having her in my past is fulfilling enough.

And you are a gift no man could ever buy. Two beautiful ladies, and two shining souls, through one set of radiant green eyes.

I GET OUT OF bed and I look through the keyhole in Mummy's bedroom door. I need to bury the book to save my mummy and my Ted from the demons. But my Ted is in there and he's making pig noises. Mummy said not to wake him up. And I can't see the book on her table with the little light on it. It's normally sitting on there next to the silver bracelet with the bits hanging off it.

Maybe my Ted buried it. Maybe my Ted just knewed that the book was full of badly and that's why he had it last night. Maybe he was taking it away. Maybe he was showing Mummy what the book will make him do if she keeps it. Maybe that's why he touched her with his foot like they did in that Karate Kid show that is coming out on the giant screen soon. Daddy said he is going to take me to see that movie. But I don't like kicking things. Only if it's me doing kicks to songs.

I like TV Hits in the weekend mornings. Mummy moves the couch back and I make up dances to the videos. I rooly rooly like that man that sings the sweet dreams are made of weeds song. I asked Mummy if all bodies really are looking for sumfing, and she said that they are. And I askted what she was looking for, and she said that she was looking for love, but she already founded it, so she's not looking anymore. I asked her to show it to me. But she said that love isn't tangible. I don't know what tangible means, but I would still like her to show me the love she found. But I stopped asking because it maded her upset and she started to cry again. I think she pretended not to cry because she kept smiling at me really weird when I was making up my sweet dreams steps.

Another reason why I don't think my mummy is very smart is because she said that the man singing that sweet dreams song was a woman! That maded me giggle. I said, she's not a woman! He has short hair, and he wears those same clothes that Daddy wears when he goes to his job, and that thing around his neck that his boss man pobably uses to show him where to go like they do with dogs. And my mummy just shookt her head and laughed at me. Silly Mummy. One day she will learn.

I want to watch TV Hits and eat brekkie. But Mummy tolded me not to wake up my Ted and it's silly to watch TV Hits without any sound on. I go into the kitchen and Mummy has left me a bowl and a box of Fruit Loops and a spoon and a bottle of milk on the kitchen table. She is smart sometimes. She did that for me so that I wouldn't have to get on a chair to get it out of the cupboard. She's nice like that. My mummy is always nice. And sometimes I think being nice, is more important than being smart.

I sit at the table and fix my brekkie. Fruit Loops are cool. But at school some kids call me a fruit loop, and I don't think they are saying it because I taste yummy. I'm not surely of what it means, but it makes me have feelings like my belly is all pineapple jelly so I don't think they are being nice to me.

My Ted is up. I hope I didn't make too much sounds with my thinking.

"Morning, sunshine. Look at you, all clever with the breakfast business."

"It's not a business. I didn't have to give money."

My Ted laughs and shakes his head.

"Where's Penny? Not like her to be out this early on a no market day."

"She's goned to Daddy's to give him a pessant."

My Ted goes on pause and his face goes flushy. And then I remember that Mummy tolded me to keep it a secret! Now I'm a bit scared and I think I go on pause too. I dribble some milk on my pyjamas by a not-on-purpose. My Ted puts his coffee cup down on the counter rooly loud and stomps back to the bedroom. I can hear all the drawings open and closing really hard. My Ted does some shouts and some rool bad words that my mummy told me to never say. Then he comes back out with his raincoat. I didn't know it was raining. But my Ted 's right. It is raining. Maybe he is smart.

"Grab your raincoat. We're going to collect her."

"Why?"

"Because she shouldn't be there."

"Why?"

"Because. You won't understand. Now just get up and get your raincoat and gumboots."

"I don't know where they are."

Ted makes funny breathing noises and wipes his mouth again. I don't understand that. He hasn't had brekkie yet. And anyway, my mummy always says that it's polite to use a serviette. When I get out of my seat Mummy opens the front door. She's smiling all nicely and unopens her umbrella and leans it against the door when she closes it.

"Oh, are you off somewhere, Ted?" That was Mummy speaking.

Ted looks like he's on pause again, except his eyes are blinking lots. Mummy's smile falls off.

"If you haven't located that *fucking* book by the time I get back all hell is going to *fucking* break loose."

"Ted! Not in front of Bonnie. You know how I feel—"

"I don't give a flying *fuck* how you feel right now."

I don't know what flying fuck means but I'm surely it's not a bird. My Ted stomps out and shuts the door rool hard and makes plates and cups go tinkle-tinkle in the cupboards. Mummy starts to cry again and she goes all wobbly to the phone. When she moves her fingers in the holes it sounds like a sleepy kitten. Sometimes I like to move my fingers in the holes and listen to it be sleepy. I want a kitten. But my Ted tolded Mummy he was a lergic. I don't know what a lergic is but it must be surely sumfing about being a man. My daddy said he's a lergic too. But he has a cat. I will ask Mrs Haydon at school what a lergic is.

Mummy goes all whisperly and she wipes her eyes with her sleeves. Then she hangs up and says that Daddy is coming over. But only for a very quickly time.

"Why?" That's me talking, not Mummy.

"He's bringing back the book."

"No! Tell him to bury the book in the ground!"

I stamp my feet rool hard on the floor, and Mummy puts her hand over her mouth rool fast. Now my chest is going all bumpy again. I don't like it when my chest is all bumpy because it makes me feel like there is a bad monster setting up a cubby in there. Mummy pulls out a chair and sits in it and sighs. She does one of those smiles that aren't happy.

"Sweetheart, that book is special. It's for me, Daddy and for you."

"But I don't want it. It's got demons in it and doors that gobble up bodies."

Mummy puts her hand on my head and I can feel it really warm and it makes me feel a bit calmed.

"There's nothing bad in the book. There is nothing to be afraid of."

I look at Mummy. I think I'm using grownup invisible words because she speaks again without any sounds coming out of my mouth first.

"Please don't feel sad, sweetie. There's no reason to feel like that at all."

"But my Ted thinks you fart in it, and that's really rude, and it's always putting tears on your face and I don't like you to be all feelings, because then all your smiles aren't happy ones anymore and I just want you to smile the happy ones and I want, I want, want … the book to *die*."

My face is really wet and I feel like the air can't find my

window. Mummy is crying rool hard now, but this time I think it was my badly, not the book's.

"Mummy, I'm sorry. I didn't want to make you sad." I let myself fall onto her lap and she grabs me and lifts me up and gives me a rooly rooly long and warmly cuddle.

"Honey, I'm not crying because I'm sad. I'm crying because I'm happy."

I rest my head on Mummy's shoulder and I think that when I'm a grownup there won't going to be any secret books.

Tape #05

Bonnie: Why do grownups make simple things go all difficultly?

Dr Wright: What do you mean?

Bonnie: They smile when they're sad and they cry when they are happy. It's silly.

Dr Wright: *[smiles]* When you grow up you'll understand a bit better why we do that.

Bonnie: I don't want to understand better. When I'm a grownup, I'm not going to do those things. I'm going to make the world simple.

Dr Wright: Really?

Bonnie: *[nods]* Uh-huh.

Dr Wright: How are you going to do that?

Bonnie: I'm not going to do silly grownup things. I'm just going to be normal. I'm not going to ask tricky questions and I'm not going to say invisible words and I'm not going to make up silly stories about the man and I'm going to be smart. Much smarter than you! *[frowns and crosses her arms in a huff]*

Dr Wright: Bonnie!

Bonnie: What?

Dr Wright: Why are you getting so upset at me? I haven't done anything bad to you.

Bonnie: You always do badly! You make me sit here with the door closed. It's not fair!

Dr Wright: Bonnie, would you prefer I open the door?

Bonnie: *[looks out window, shakes head]*

Dr Wright: Bonnie? Would you like to try some writing?

Bonnie: *[shakes head]*

Dr Wright: Not real writing. You can spell words with these wooden letters. Would that be fun?

Bonnie: *[looks at box of letters, shrugs]*

Dr Wright: Look. I'll start. *[empties letters onto table and spells own name: Doctor Wright.]* Do you know what I've spelt?

Bonnie: Yes. I'm not stupid.

Dr Wright: Okay, would you like to read it to me?

Bonnie: It says Doctor Wright.

Dr Wright: Wow! That's fantastic, Bonnie. Who's been teaching you about silent letters?

Bonnie: Daddy. Because Daddy is smart.
Dr Wright: And so are you, Bonnie. That's brilliant. Bravo. *[claps hands]*
Bonnie: *[smiles and takes some letters out of the box. She spells: Silent letters are stupid.]*

THE DOORBELL RINGS AND it's Daddy. Mummy takes her hair out of the flicky-band and puts her fingers through it before she opens the door.

When she opens the door, they both go on pause. Except Daddy's lip. It moves funny. Like someone is pulling it by a string. He's holding the book. I still think it's got badly things in it, but if it makes Daddy come visit, then maybe sometimes it might be okay. Maybe when those some times happen the demons are sleeping and the doors are lockted.

Daddy looks at me and blinks at me with one eye. Then he touches Mummy's cheek and she pushes her face into his hand a bit more. Mummy goes outside and closes the front door. I can see their lips moving but I can't hear them, not even whisperlies. But I *can* still see them through the window. My mummy isn't smart like that, but Daddy is, but maybe he's forgotten about that window because he isn't living with us anymore.

I'm glad there is a window because I just sawed them touching lips. And when I touch my lips to Mummy's lips it make me feel warm. It's good she is touching Daddy's lips because it's not being summer today and he doesn't have a raincoat.

February 19th, 1984
~Mummy

I will never forget yesterday morning. John kissed me when he brought this book back (just in the nick of time, too, before Ted came home to find out what I had done, so I guess he's also a saviour). We didn't say much. But I think it might be a new beginning. I don't want to pressure him, so I won't ask any questions. Let's just see how it pans out. This will be the first time in my life that I will "go with the flow." Bonnie, wish me luck. I need it!

Bonnie, remember, no matter how old you are, you never stop learning.

Ted and I had a big "conversation" last night. He wants me to focus on bringing the three of us closer together. He asked if he could start writing in the book too. I told him that it wouldn't be right, seeing as John started it. I said that I thought it would be betraying him somehow. And it would. Don't you think? Anyway, I promised Ted that I would stop writing in it. That I would give it to John. Ted seemed to find that solution acceptable.

Now, I need to find a place to hide this book.

John and I are meeting in the park tomorrow for me to give him the book. I'll pick you up from school and we can walk there together.

PS: We put the Talking Heads album on this morning and you made up a really innovative dance to Burning Down the House. You said that you thought the lyrics didn't make sense. I asked you why, and you said that you can't put out a fire with fire, and that a fire doesn't make you wet so why would you need a raincoat? I tried to explain that the lyrics are like art and that they don't have to make sense, but you wouldn't have it. Then you lifted your shoulders to your ears, sighed, and said, "Well, at least I can dance to it." Ted laughed. A real belly laugh. It was nice to see him laugh for a change.

PPS: I hope John reads my entries.

Tape #06

Bonnie: *[jumps up and down on the couch like a trampoline]*
Dr Wright: Bonnie, I know it's fun, but you might break the couch.
Bonnie: I won't break the couch!
Dr Wright: You might.
Bonnie: I'm too small. I'm not heavy.
Dr Wright: I know that, but when you jump up and down like that, you become heavier than you really are.
Bonnie: That doesn't make logic.
Dr Wright: Why doesn't it make sense, Bonnie?
Bonnie: I can't be growing just because I'm jumping. You're really silly. I'm not growing taller. It just looks like it.
Dr Wright: *[shakes head and laughs]*
Bonnie: *[stops jumping]* Why do grownups shake their heads a lot like they are saying no but not really saying no?
Dr Wright: Why do you think we shake our heads, Bonnie?
Bonnie: *[shrugs]* Maybe you are making surely the nits don't get in. Maybe that's why kids get nits a lot, because they're always nodding at the grownup questions.

Dr Wright: *[smiles]* That's a pretty good theory, Bonnie. Where did you hear that?

Bonnie: What?

Dr Wright: *[laughs]*

Bonnie: I wasn't saying a joke.

Dr Wright: Bonnie?

Bonnie: What?

Dr Wright: You're amazing.

Bonnie: *[nods, smiles]* I know.

IT'S BEING SUMMER AGAIN today and I'm playing on the swing set my Ted got me for my birthday. He said five was a very special age because five is when you start school. I started school. But I don't feel special. I think it's because I'm a fruit loop. Sara and Bianca are meanies and I don't like them anymore. And there is a boy at school with red hair. His name is Albert and his face looks like a porcipontus. He has a yucky voice and when he calls me a fruit loop it sounds like a body put him in a morning blender with I-scream and milk. I think bodies should call him the fruit loop, not me.

And I'm not stupid. But some bodies think I'm stupid. I think Dr Right thinks I'm stupid too. She said that I was borned too early and that means that I don't learn very fast. Maybe I don't spell very good, but I can write and I can read and I can dance, and I know there's rooly no moon man, and I can understand grownup invisible words.

I think some words are spelled silly because they aren't spelled like you say them. I told Dr Right, but she just said I have to learn the way they are spelled in the dickshonary. I know how they are spelled in the dickshonary. I just like my spelled words better.

When I'm growed up I will make a new dickshonary and all the words in it will be spelled the way we say them. One of the stupid spellings is when there are letters that you don't say. Like *lamb*. It's stupid to have the b there. And like *know*. That k is stupid too. The body that invented those stupid silent letters must have beened the one who invented grownup invisible words. Maybe there isn't any histories of him because he didn't want any bodies to see him. And that's another thing I don't understand. Why do all the boys get the stories? There should be herstories too. I've got lots of them and I'm a girl.

There's a girl in my classroom that should have a herstory. She always hides behind the shelter shed at recess and says she's to be invisible. When I go to speak to her she runs away. I wish she would speak to me. Because Sara and Bianca don't like me anymore. I know that because they started to be calling me a fruit loop too.

That's another stupid spelling. Fruit. Maybe that's why my Ted isn't very smart because he works with fruit. My mummy would tell me not to use the word stupid, and to use silly instead. But I like the word stupid. So I'll just make it an invisible word and use it when I'm thinking only.

Mummy is coming outside with a biscuit tin. I don't think she knows I'm on the swing. She looks into the sky with the biscuit tin cuddled under her chin. She says some words to the sky with her eyes closed but I can't hear them. Then she puts the biscuit tin on the ground and goes into the garage and brings out the rooly heavy shaker stick, but the one that doesn't have the gaps. She starts poking it into the dirt under the bush with the nice smelling white flowers all over it and makes a big hole. She puts a plastic super bag in the hole and pushes it down like she does with biscuit dough. Then she puts the biscuit tin in it. Maybe she wants to hide the biscuits from me because she says I eat too many sweets.

But it doesn't matter, when I go visit Daddy, Mary will give me Tim Tams.

***

Mrs Haydon is making us wear these stupid smocks. Mine is too big and I hate the colour. It looks like poo in my undies. Mrs Haydon is making us do finger-painting on big pieces of paper clipped to a big wood thing. And the paint colours are boring. There is just yellow, blue, red and boring old white. I thought Mrs Haydon was smart because she's a teacher, but how does she not know that if I put white paint on white paper, that no one is rooly going to see it?

I put my hand up to get more colours because that's what we're supposed to do when we have a question. But she doesn't come over and my arm is getting sore and feels all wobbly like pineapple jelly. I can hear her talking in her witch voice to Bianca. Maybe she told Mrs Haydon that I'm a fruit loop and now Mrs Haydon doesn't like me anymore either. So I get up and go to the cupboard with the paints in it myself and there isn't any green in there either!

"I want to make *trees*." That was me, saying it rool loud

so Mrs Haydon can hear and would stop hearing lies from Bianca and come over to me. Now she comes over, but she's got grumpy lines on her head and says in her witchy voice that I can make trees if I want to.

"But trees are *green*, stupid. There's no green!" That's me yelling again. I don't think I should be yelling at Mrs Haydon. My mummy tolded me that I should respect Mrs Haydon, and that means to speak nicely. Mrs Haydon's eyes go all googly and shiny and she puts her hands on her hips and her lip does that thing like it did with Daddy's like it's being pulled by a string.

"Apologize for your foul use of language and your inappropriate tone, young lady, or I'll take you straight up to the Principal's office. Would you like to go to the Principal's office?"

Teachers ask tricky questions too. They ask questions about things that they already know we don't want. I don't think that makes logic.

I put my head down and look at my shoes. "I'm sorry, Mrs Haydon." I already knewed that I should only say stupid when I'm thinking, but I said it out loud. That was stupid.

"Now, if you have a little patience, my dear, I can show you how to make some green. Do you have a little patience?"

I nod. But I can't tell if this is a Daddy type question or a my Ted type question. But it doesn't matter. If Mrs Haydon can make me some green, then I can paint some trees.

We walk to my big wood thing and Mrs Haydon smiles

like she's about to be naughty. She dips the paint brush in the yellow, and rubs it onto the plastic lunch box lid. Then she dips the paint brush into the water and then into the blue and rubs that onto the yellow. She moves the paintbrush around in the paint and the paint turns green!

I can't believe it! Maybe Mrs Haydon rooly is a witch, but a good witch pretending to be a bad witch, so that the bad witches don't turn her into a mouse.

Daddy says that you learn something new every day. But I bet he's never learnted how to make magic colours!

***

WHEN MUMMY MEETS ME at the school gate she tells me we're going to meet Daddy in the park and that gives me fizzy feelings in my Mr Stomach. I wonder if he will be getting me an I-scream. I want a rainbow one today. The ones that look like rainbows make me suck my cheeks in because some of the colours are sour like lemons. I don't like lemons, but I like rainbow I-scream.

When we get there I give Daddy a big hug and he gives me a big hug back. Mummy is holding the book with the demons and I hope that the doors are still lockted so that Daddy doesn't kick Mummy like my Ted did.

When Daddy and I stop hugging she gives it to him. They touch hands for a rooly long time behind Daddy's back. I think they think that I don't see it, but I can. I can't but somehow I'm thinking I can. Maybe Mrs Haydon gave me some magic powers for the day because I painted the best thing in the class and she put it up on the classroom wall.

Maybe my mummy's not-smartness travels to my daddy when they touch. Maybe that's how bodies fall in love. I've hearded that word so many times on TV Hits, and all bodies in my family say that to each other. And Mummy had splained it to me one time, but I still don't think I understand how it works.

That makes me remember, I should ask her to show me the love that she founded a long time ago. Maybe I can understand it better when I see it. I was going to ask Mrs Haydon, but I felted a bit shy after she did the magic colours. She made me orange and purple and pink too. Now I know why she gave us white! I didn't want to ask too many more favours after that. Because Daddy said doing that is "over-stepping the mark." He splained what it meanted. I didn't see any mark on the ground when Mrs Haydon was doing the colour magic. But then I thought of Mrs Haydon telling me to have a little patience, and I thoughted I should listen because teachers know what's good for kids more than kids.

The wind blows and it makes my arms feel funny. My arms go all dotted and my hairs like tiny feathers. Mummy and Daddy are all whisperly so no-one can hear their secrets.

"I didn't read it. But it was torture." That was Mummy, not Daddy.

Daddy smiles and touches Mummy's cheek with a word like gentle. I learnted that word today when Mrs Haydon tolded me to press the paint brushes down gentle so that the line didn't go so thick. Mrs Haydon is very smart.

I don't think my Ted would be happy to see Daddy touch Mummy with the gentle word. Mummy tolded me that when two bodies go to a church to say their vows, that you're not allowed to give love to another body else. But I don't think I can say what I think until Mummy gives the love to me to hold.

Daddy makes funny eyes at Mummy like he's asking an invisible question and Mummy nods, and then nods at me.

"Would you like to come and stay with Mary and me tonight? I can drop you off to school on the way to work in the morning." That was Daddy speaking.

Daddy does a blink with one eye to Mummy, and Mummy smiles a happy one.

"That sounds like a fun idea, doesn't it, Bonnie?" That's my mummy, not Daddy.

It looks like they are having invisible talking again, like Daddy did with Mary, but this time he doesn't look annoyed.

Mummy whispers, "You can keep her for two nights if you like."

He smiles a rooly rooly big one and I can see his teeth. "You sure?"

Mummy nods and points her chin to the book and lifts the eyebrows above her eyes.

Daddy smiles and shakes his head and nods and shakes his head. I don't think he knows what he's saying. Maybe he hasn't learnted the invisible language as good as Mummy and my Ted yet.

"Sweetheart, would you like to go and play on the slide for a while? Daddy and I have to discuss something in private. We'll just be right over here." Mummy points to the long wood seat that fits bodies like a couch, and I nod to answer that question that is like a trick and walk over to the slide. But I don't go on the slide because every time I go on the slide my bum goes all burny on the skin and it stings a lot.

I sit under the slide and play with the bark. The sun is hiding a bit now and I'm feeling a bit shaky, but not too shaky. I watch my mummy and my daddy smiling the happy way. That's good. I think they are learning to do things poperly instead of the wrong way around now. Maybe Dr Right has been helping them to be learning too.

But then my Daddy stands up rooly fast and runs behind the trees on the other side of the playground. My mummy is looking left and right and left again, like she is going to cross the road, but rooly rooly fast. My heart is going all bumpy because I think sumfing is wrong, but then I think they're just playing hide and seek! So I get up and run towards Mummy because I want to play too, and I call out, "I know where he is! He's behind the tree! Let's go and find him together, Mummy!" And then my Ted says, "Find who, Bonnie? Who's behind the tree?" And I look up and it's my Ted, but his face is all faded because it's trying to be summer again and the sun is poking in my eyes.

"Hi Ted!" That's me saying hi in a rooly high voice and I feel like giggling because now the four of us can play together and it will be *so* fun like Supercalifragilisticexpialidocious. And then I say, "It's—" but then Mummy laughs rooly rooly loud but it doesn't sound like her popper laugh, and she says to my Ted rooly loud that I have an imaginary friend, and that makes me rooly angry because I'm not a crazy body, I'm smart, I go to school, I know that imaginary friends are just in books and I want to yell that Mummy is lying but then she looks at me rooly tough like I've never ever seen her look at me before, and my Ted huffs and puts his hands on his hips and squints into the sky and says, "How about we take the afternoon and go to the beach before the weather starts crapping out, hey?"

I don't know what crapping out means, but I don't think it means sumfing good. I want to say that I want to go home with Daddy who is waiting for me in the trees, so that I can get my rainbow I-scream, but sumfing makes me feel like Mummy would get madly if I did that.

"That's a fabulous idea, Ted." That was Mummy sounding all excited but she's not rooly. She looks at the tree where Daddy is hiding and I wave to him and Mummy smacks my hand down and it hurts. I make an *ow* and Mummy does a shooshing. It looks like my Ted doesn't see Daddy. My mummy does doll's eyes and we follow my Ted to the car.

My mummy is being a bit silly. I think I understand the words Daddy and Mummy are doing all whisperly now. And that makes my Ted even sillier.

My Ted is a Mr Grumpy. But I don't think he is a baddie like in the movies with the violence. I don't want to give him hugs like I want to give to my mummy. But there might be another girl somewhere who does want to give him hugs. And I think my mummy should tell him to go and find another body to live with if she doesn't like him anymore. I think my mummy is being a meanie like Sara and Bianca. And that makes me wish my Ted to get a zillion hugs.

February 21st, 1984
~Daddy

This is such unacceptable behaviour on our parts, Bonnie. That was a really close call at the park yesterday and I'm sorry you had to be witness to that. I'm sure it confused you to no end. And I wouldn't put it past you if you completely comprehended what was going on.

You are a very intelligent young lady. Which means that one day you will understand why we do the things we do. Our foolish actions may seem selfish to you now. But when you love someone, it feels like the rest of the world has no right to exist. I hope one day you are granted this gift—this wonderful gift of love.

Bonnie, Penny and I have a plan. I'm not sure I will be seeing you very often anymore. But it's only temporary. I'm sorry we are being so secretive, but it's for your own good. If Penny and I let our feelings for each other get in the way of making our past wrongs into rights, then the result will be catastrophic for you, especially at such an influential age, my love. Please don't be upset with me. Daddy loves you.

Always.

part three

love is tangible

Tape #07

Bonnie: Why is that wood stuff in the park ground called like the dog sound? It doesn't make logic.

Dr Wright: Some things don't make much sense, but it doesn't mean they are incorrect.

Bonnie: *[blank stare]*

Dr Wright: You look upset today, Bonnie.

Bonnie: *[crosses arms and huffs]*

Dr Wright: Would you like to tell me what's wrong?

Bonnie: *[shakes head]*

Dr Wright: Why not?

Bonnie: Because it's none of your beeswax.

Dr Wright: Everything in this room stays between us. You know that, don't you?

Bonnie: Words can't stick between bodies. They go out of mouths and into the air and float around like songs.

Dr Wright: That's very insightful, Bonnie.

Bonnie: *[blank stare]*

Dr Wright: I won't tell anyone what you tell me. I promise. Is something happening at home that is bothering you?

Bonnie: *[shakes head]*

Dr Wright: Are you sure?

Bonnie: *[frowns]*

Dr Wright: We can sit here in silence until you're ready to talk to me, Bonnie. But I'm not letting you go home until you tell me what's going on.

Bonnie: *[falls into couch and buries her head into cushions]*

Dr Wright: Mummy showed me a really fantastic picture you made with macaroni at school. I'd like to hang one just like it on my wall. Would you make one for me?

Bonnie: *[screams into cushion]*

Dr Wright: Bonnie, if you don't start behaving yourself, I'm going to have to let you go home without any jellybeans today.

Bonnie: *[sits up, wipes eyes, looks out the window]* Mummy won't let me hold her love.

Mummy has stopped to cry when my Ted goes to the shop without her. I think that's because she has stopped to write in the book. I *knew* the book was the badly!

But now I'm madly at Daddy because he only talks to me on the phone. He said that he's sorry I can't come over to play, but that he has to look after Mary. It doesn't make logic. Mary knows how to pretend to be a grownup. She doesn't need to play with Daddy. But I do. It's not fair!

But I think it's good that Mummy isn't doing sillies with Daddy anymore. Because my Ted "deserves better". That's a thing what Mummy said when she sawed a TV show about the Youth in Asia. It was sumfing about how they should be able to choose when to die if they are really sick. There must be a lot of sick kids in that country if they are going to let them make themselves to die. I hope they go to heaven.

I think Mummy is becoming smart. Because she smiles a lot now and the smiles are happy and the way they're supposed to be. And she hasn't beened happy crying either. Daddy is right. You do learn sumfing new every day. Even grownups who pobably know almost everything already like Mrs Haydon and Dr Right.

My Ted brought me home sumfing called a custard apple. And I asked him to give the list of things to buy from the super for Mummy to make some more because they tasted rool yummy. My Ted laughed at me again. He said that custard apples are a plant and they grow to taste that yummy. But that doesn't make logic. I sawed Mrs Haydon make toffee apples at the fete and the toffee was maded by her!

I think that the fruit is making my Ted a bit more not-smart.

It think that my Ted might be a fruit loop.

April 19th, 1984
~Mummy

John said that it shouldn't be long now before he finds Mary a flat. She's old enough to live on her own now, and it seems they have given up hope regarding Mary's mother getting her memory back. John said that once Mary moves out that we can move back in with him! Won't that be so great?!

Ted still doesn't know we've been meeting in the park to exchange the book. And he doesn't know our plans either. I can't break it to him yet. If I did he would probably throw us out on the street, and then what would we do? No, it's best that it stays a secret until we can make this a reality. I know this is not a good example for you, and when you read this, please don't think that this behaviour is accept-able. It's not. But things are hard for me. I don't have any skills. I've never had a job. I wouldn't be able to afford to support you without Ted's help.

His business is going a lot better lately. So his mood has changed somewhat. Which is just wonderful for us and such good timing too. But it's probably more to do with him believing I've given up on the book. He's such a jealous man. I only write in it now when he's at the shop and you're at school. When I'm here all alone. When I'm finished, I hide it in an Arnott's Assorted Biscuits tin and bury it in the backyard under the big jasmine bush. It's safer that way.

Everything is safer when you keep secrets.

One day, you'll learn that secrets are sometimes one's only saviour. The only thing I deeply regret about this is how much it's going to hurt Ted. He has been such a good father to you, and I'm such a horrible wife. I owe him so much.

I wish I could make it quick and painless for him. Like ripping off a Band-Aid. If only life were that simple, Bonnie. I truly hope that when you grow up you fall in love and stay in love and that life remains as simple as it should be. Of course, there will always be complications, but if you truly love someone, I hope this book will be a constant reminder to never give up hope. If you are meant to be together, things will work out for the best in the end.

Anyway, enough of this melancholia.

Guess what it is this Sunday? Easter! Boy do I have a surprise for you.

I THINK I HAD in-some-knee-ah because my Ted and my mummy said I get to go on an egg hunt this morning in the backyard! It's Easter Sunday today and yesterday I got to paint eggs with my Ted and Mummy and Daddy and Mary. I think my Ted and Daddy are friends now and I think that's rooly good. Now we can all be a rooly happy big family and I can have two daddies and a big sister too!

I showeded Mary how to make magic colours. She was all surprised, and she put her hand to her mouth and went "oh wow" rool loud and started doing some weird dance-jumping around the kitchen and saying silly things like abracadabra and wazzam-wazzoo Jackaroo.

I think she already knewed about the colour magic. I don't understand why grownups pretend to be surprised about things around kids. I was going to tell her that I knewed she was pretending but she was having so much fun so I pretended to be excited about her being excited and then we was both rooly happy making magic colours and painting the eggs.

Daddy and Mary are coming over again this morning to do the egg hunt thing with me. I'm so excited, it's going to be the best day in the whole wide world. I wanted Mummy to play too but she said she is going to be hiding the eggs so she can't play. I said why not and she said because she will know where they are. I think my mummy is getting more smart because I didn't think of that and I'm really smart.

I can hear noises in the bathroom now, so I think my mummy or my Ted is gotten up. Then my mummy goes all singy-songy with my name in the hall.

"Bonnie, Connie, Von Wommie, bam, wam, can, Bonnie," and she starts making drums on the walls and then she runs into my bedroom and jumps on my bed and goes all tickling me!

I'm giggling rool loud and she's making roaring noises like a lion with courage which is silly because it's Easter. She should be going *brrk! brrk!* like a chicken, and just then like she sawed my thinking thoughts she starts to go *brrk! brrk!* like a chicken and flicking her elbows out and in and it looks *so* funny, specially when she goes all gobbeldy with her head backwards and forwards. She looks so silly!

"Mummy you look so silly!"

"Good morning, Bonnie!" That was my mummy in a chicken voice that sounds like she has chopsticks up her nose. "Are you ready, *brrrk!*, to cluck around the garden of, *brrrk!*, glorious chocolate heaven?"

She's making me laugh and I'm laughing rool loud.

"This is serious, *brrrk!*, business my child, you have some serious, *brrrk!*, hunting to do, *brrrk!*, my little chickie dee." Mummy does her chook movements even bigger now and it looks like she is going to cluck her arms and head off. I'm laughing rool hard now and my breath is going funny and I'm making noises like Little Miss Piggy. Then Mummy goes all floppy and falls on my bed and makes a big sigh with her eyes closed. She has a big happy smile and she lies next to me and grabs me tight in her arms and kisses me *all* over my head and my eyes and my mouth and my nose and hair bits that go up and down when people talk.

"I love you so much, sweetheart." That was my mummy, not me. I never called Mummy sweetheart before, but I do say I love you to her. And that makes me think of the question I was going to ask.

"Mummy, can you show me the love you found now?"

"I am showing you the love, sweetie."

"Where is it?"

"It's here."

"Where?"

Mummy makes a big sigh and says, "The love is right here between us. You can't hold it like a ball. It's something you feel. Just like you feel now about me, and I feel about you."

"But you said that you *found* love. How can you *find* sumfing you can't hold in your hand?"

Mummy makes a funny noise through her nose. She does those funny noises a lot lately.

"Darling, you tell Daddy and Ted and me that you love us all the time. Are you holding love in your hand when you say that? No, you're not. You're feeling it, aren't you?"

This makes me think and I go *um* and look up at the roof and I would be looking into the sky at the clouds if I was outside.

And then I understand what she is asking and I say, "No, I just say it to you because you say it to me."

Mummy laughs and does more animal noises and shakes me with the gentle word a bit and hugs me a bit more tightly.

"Darling, you will understand it better when you get older. I promise."

"But I want to understand *now*!" That's me getting louder with my speaking. I know it's rude to get loud with speaking but I can't help it.

"Okay, Bonnie. Listen. How about we get you dressed and washed up, then we can do the egg hunt, and then we can talk about what love is as a whole family at the table when we eat lunch?"

I'm going to say no when Mummy breathes in rool quick and says, "Did you hear that?"

"What?" My ears go prick like a dog, I think.

"That's the sound of Daddy and Mary. Quick, up you get, put on your dressing gown and go wash your face, and then we can start the egg hunt."

"Okay." That's me getting up and putting my dressing gown on so I can go hunt for chocolate eggs with Daddy and Mary and my Ted in the garden.

This is going to be the best day in my whole entire life. And guess what? I sawed some rooly pretty butterflies in the garden yesterday and I decided I'm going to catch one in a jar and Daddy said that he's going to teach me rool interesting things about them. It's fun when Daddy teaches me things. I think he's better than Dr Right and Mrs Haydon.

I think Daddy should be a teacher.

IN THE GARDEN MUMMY has put lots of little baskets with lots of little yellow chicks and pink bunnies, and I said to her that she was supposed to hide them not just put them around the garden, and she says that she did hide them you silly duffer, and that the baskets are there to put the eggs into when I find them and that makes me think and I think that it makes good logic.

Daddy and Mary and my Ted and me all look in different places in the garden and Mummy is calling out funny stuff that doesn't make logic.

"Ted you're warm! John you're really cold! Mary you're getting warmer! Bonnie you're getting hot! Good girl!"

"I'm not hot. I'm just warm." That was me yelling so Mummy can hear me over her loudness. And everybody laughs at the same time and that makes me cry because it gives me sticky feelings in my belly like pineapple jelly like when Sara and Bianca call me a fruit loop at school.

Mary comes over to me and pats my head like I'm a kitten and then gives me a hug. She smells like pretty flowers today and that makes me feel a bit more calmed.

"Don't cry, Bonnie." That's Mary being nice all whisperly. "That's just what you say when someone is getting closer to finding the treasure. It's a good thing. It means that you are really close to finding some eggs. When someone is cold, it means they are far away. When someone is hot, it means they are really close. And you are really close!"

This makes me think and I think it doesn't make logic. But I have learnted that English is silly and doesn't make logic most of the time, so I think I just have to be learning to like all the unlogic stuff.

Mary wipes my tears away with her sleeve and I sniff and nod.

"Can you give me a smile?" That is a nice trick question. I like Mary sometimes.

I smile and nod and go to look inside the grasses behind the plum tree because that's where I am and Mummy said I'm hot and that means I'm close to the treasure. And when I move some of the grasses to the side I can see some silvery blue purpled shinies! I reach in and I pick up three little chocolate eggs and I hold them above my head and I scream "Eureka!" because I learnted in school that some man in histories said this when he found sumfing rooly important and that in some other language, I forget which one, that the word means "I found it."

And then after I say that really smart word all bodies in my backyard start to clap and yell hurrahs and I do a funny dance and Mary does it with me. Mary is funny sometimes. But then my Ted does a loud noise with his throat and everyone except me and Mary goes on pause. My Ted is holding the biscuit box my mummy did a pray to the sky with.

"Mummy put the biscuits there so I couldn't eat them."

That's me talking so that my Ted can understand why there's biscuits buried in the garden.

But my Ted opens the biscuit box and pulls out the book! The *badly* book! I want to yell out *no*! and take it away and throw it over the fence to the horribly lady next door, but my voice is gone and I don't know where to look for it. Ted's face is all red and shiny and his breathing is all loud, and Mummy and Daddy move next to each other, and Daddy looks at Mummy's shoes again and puts his arm around her shoulders. Mummy has both hands over her mouth and there's tears falling down her face, and then she whispers my Ted's name.

My Ted opens the book and it looks like he's reading invisible words and then after a minute he chucks the book at my daddy and it hits him in the face. My mummy yells, "Ted! How dare you!" rool loud and it makes me put my hands to my ears. But Daddy is rooly quick and he catches the book and holds it to his chest and hugs Mummy into him a bit more tightly.

"When were you going to fucking tell me about this, this … this cold-hearted plan of yours, huh? You stupid fucking bitch. How long has this been fucking going on?" That was my Ted and he's speaking rool loud and he's saying rool bad words and the horribly lady over the fence yells out to shut the fuck up arseholes. I think that word means bottom, but I'm not surely.

"Ted, I, I, I—" That was Mummy and I think she has lost her voice too. It's all the book's badly, the book has to go in the fire and *not* get a raincoat!

Then my Ted does sumfing really violent. He stomps up to my mummy and punches her in the face! Then my Daddy punches my Ted and I can see blood coming out of his nose and there's a lot of yelling and screaming and punching, and Mary isn't doing *any*thing, she's just standing there holding my basket of eggs and my legs start going all rattling and my heart all bumpy in my chest rool hard, and then I can feel my voice comes back rool loud and I scream and scream and scream and run to Daddy and Mummy and my Ted and I yell for them to stop doing hurting that it's *not* nice and to stop, *please* Daddy, Mummy, stop stop *stop*!!!

And then all bodies in the backyard go on pause except for the oxygen. My mummy is on the ground holding her hands over her eyes and crying rool lots and my daddy and my Ted are touching the red on their faces and Mary is making crying sounds but rool quietly like she wants to be invisible.

It's all the book's badly, but it's my mummy's badly too because she didn't listen to me when I told her it has demons in it. And I don't know why, it doesn't make much logic, but I get this rooly badly feeling in my tummy and my chest and my head and my face goes all burning and I scream rool loud at my mummy, "I HATE YOU! I HATE YOU! I HATE YOU!"

And I run down the driveway rool fast and I can hear my mummy and my daddy and my Ted call my name but it sounds so far away inside my oxygen and my bumpy heart in my ears, and I run and run and run and I get to the road and I don't stop and then I can hear a rooly loud horn like they blow at the beginning of the Melbourne Cup and and and then I hear a really big bang-clang and a loudly screeching and screaming so loud that I've never heard noises so big before and then everything goes magic colours and I can hear more screams and crying and big heavy feet around me.

Then the world goes a big black.

Bonnie ... I don't think I can do this. I'm devastated. I'm sorry. I'm sorry that I didn't let you hold love ...

April 28th, 1984
~Daddy

My precious Bonnie,

The doctors said you didn't feel any pain. I think the world gave it all to Penny and I. I am thankful for that. I am thankful that you were spared a horrific death. But one thing I am not thankful for is that you had to leave us with so many unanswered questions.

Dr Wright gave us your session tapes. We can't stop watching and listening to you. I think Penny is going to make herself sick with them, but I can't bear to take them away from her. If I try to turn the VCR off she becomes hysterical. She hasn't spoken for days. She's tried so many times to write you a goodbye letter, but every time she picks up this book she breaks down. So I think it's best if I write for the both of us.

I promised Penny I'd give you all the answers you've been hoping for:

1. It's called ice cream because it's made of ice and cream. But I do agree with your magnificent logic that they should be called I-quiets. It's the only food I want to enjoy in complete silence too.

2. Mary is not more special than you. I love you the same and sometimes oh so much more.

3. Sometimes grownups don't say what they're thinking because they don't want to hurt someone's feelings. But you are right. We should all say what we are thinking. We should all say the truth. Invisible words are bad. The world would be a better place if we had the courage to get all our thoughts out in the open, and if you had the chance to grow up big, I think you would have made a perfect mother.

4. Ted calls you a young lady because you are just as intelligent as any of us. If not, more so.

5. Mummy liked to think the man on the moon was real because a thought like that sounds magical. She knew it wasn't really real. Just like you knew that the Easter Bunny wasn't real. But to pretend that they are real, makes life so much more fun.

6. Sometimes grownups ask questions that don't need answering because, to be frank, as you get older, you become more selfish and believe that you have the right to get your own way all the time. I suppose you are lucky to have left us when life still seemed bigger than yourself.

7. Grownups shake their heads a lot because some things still surprise us. Even though we like to believe we know everything, we don't. We are just children in grownup skin.

8. Why do grownups make simple things so difficult? I don't know. I'd really like to know the answer to that one

myself. I wish you could have grown up to be a beautiful woman, and find the answer to that very important and intelligent question. We could all do with a bit of simplicity in this life.

9. It is silly that the stuff on the ground in the park is called the same as the voice of a dog, isn't it? I couldn't agree with you more. There are always going to be things in life that people don't like, or even understand. But if you don't learn to accept them the way that they are, and this goes for people too, you will never feel true happiness. That's something I have learned from you, Bonnie. Thank you.

10. And lastly, now this is the most important one, are you listening? It turns out that you can hold love like a ball. You were right all along. But it's not the shape of a ball, it's the shape of a book. This book. And tomorrow, my love, I will put it in your hands, before we put you in the earth. The earth that gifted me with the most beautiful thing in the world. You, Bonnie my love.

Only you.

acknowledgements

When I was a child, my mother, Erika Bach, and my father, Anthony Bell, wrote in an illustrated journal by Michael Green called *A Hobbit's Travels: being the hitherto unpublished Travel Sketches of Sam Gamgee.* This journal is the inspiration for this book. Thank you for keeping it, and blessing me with such an amazing treasure. It will always have a special place on my bookshelf.

I must also add that in Part One of this book, there are some excerpts that are used verbatim. Thank you for your permission to do this. Without your precious words, this book would not exist.

I must also thank my editors, Dawn Ius and Leigh T. Moore, for their insights and expertise in helping me make *The Book* the best it could possibly be, and to Stacey Larner for her sound advice regarding Bonnie's voice.

And of course, a very special thanks to Amie McCracken for her enormous help in producing *The Bell Collection* edition.

Enjoyed this book?
Go to *vineleavespress.com/books*
to find more from *The Bell Collection*.

To sign up to Jessica's newsletter
and/or connect with her on social media
go to *jessicabellauthor.com/contact*.

Are you a writer?
You might be interested in Jessica's
Writing in a Nutshell series.